# ★ LONG TIME, ★
# NO SEA MONSTER

★ Also in the ★
MS. FROGBOTTOM'S FIELD TRIPS series

Book 1: *I Want My Mummy!*

COMING SOON:
Book 3: *Fangs for Having Us!*

# MS. FROGBOTTOM'S FIELD TRIPS

★ LONG TIME, NO SEA MONSTER ★

By **OLiVER**, *as told to* **NaNCY KRULiK**
*Illustrated by* **HaRRY BRIGGS**

## ALADDIN

New York   London   Toronto   Sydney   New Delhi

ALADDIN

An imprint of Simon & Schuster Children's Publishing Division

1230 Avenue of the Americas, New York, New York 10020

First Aladdin hardcover edition April 2021

Text copyright © 2021 by Nancy Krulik

Illustrations copyright © 2021 by Harry Briggs

Also available in an Aladdin paperback edition.

All rights reserved, including the right of reproduction in whole or in part in any form.

ALADDIN and related logo are registered trademarks of Simon & Schuster, Inc.

For information about special discounts for bulk purchases, please contact Simon & Schuster Special Sales at 1-866-506-1949 or business@simonandschuster.com.

The Simon & Schuster Speakers Bureau can bring authors to your live event.

For more information or to book an event contact the Simon & Schuster Speakers Bureau at 1-866-248-3049 or visit our website at www.simonspeakers.com.

Jacket designed by Karin Paprocki

Interior designed by Mike Rosamilia

The illustrations for this book were rendered digitally.

The text of this book was set in Neutraface Slab Text.

Manufactured in the United States of America 0321 FFG

2 4 6 8 10 9 7 5 3 1

Library of Congress Control Number 2020936865

ISBN 9781534454002 (hc)

ISBN 9781534453999 (pbk)

ISBN 9781534454019 (ebook)

For Danny, who goes
wherever the music takes him
—N. K.

# WELCOME TO CLASS 4A.

We have a warning for you:

**BEWARE OF THE MAP.**

Our classroom probably looks a lot like yours. We have chairs, desks, a whiteboard, and artwork on the walls. And of course we have our teacher, Ms. Frogbottom.

Actually, our teacher is the reason why things sometimes get strange

★ 1 ★

around here. Because Ms. Frogbottom is kind of *different*.

For starters, she carries around a backpack. It looks like any other pack, but somehow strange things always seem to be popping out of it. You don't have to worry about most of the stuff our teacher carries. But if she reaches into her pack and pulls out her giant map, beware. That map is *magic*. It has the power to lift us right out of our classroom and drop us in some faraway place. And somehow it's always the same exact time as when we left. No matter where we go, we wind up meeting frightening creatures none of us ever believed were real—and getting into all sorts of trouble.

You don't have to be *too* scared, though. Things always seem to turn out okay for us in the end. Or at least they have *so far*. . . .

Your new pals,

Aiden, Emma, Oliver, Olivia, Sofia, and Tony

# MS. FROGBOTTOM'S FiELD TRiP DO'S aND DON'TS

- Do stay together.

- Don't take photos. You can't experience the big world through a tiny camera hole.

- Don't bring home souvenirs. We want to leave the places we visit exactly as we found them.

- Don't use the word "weird." The people, places, and food we experience are just different from what you are used to.

- Do have fun!

**_La, La, La, La, La._**

Have you ever seen what little kids do when they don't want to hear something? They stick their fingers into their ears and start singing really loudly.

_La, la, la, la, la._

I wish I could do that now, because I don't want to listen to Emma and Aiden fighting anymore.

But I'm _not_ a little kid. I'm in fourth

grade. And that's waaaayyy too big to stick your fingers into your ears.

Besides, I haven't cleaned my ears for a while. It could be kind of gross in there.

"Oliver! Are you listening to me?" Emma sticks her face in front of mine.

"I've *been* listening to you," I assure her.

"My dance recital should be on the

front page of the 4A *Gazette*," Emma tells me. "If you were a real newspaper editor, you'd know that."

Emma's been saying things like that for the past fifteen minutes.

"My flag football game belongs on the front page," Aiden argues. "We're in the playoffs!"

Aiden's been saying things like *that* for the past fifteen minutes.

See what I mean about wanting to stick my fingers into my ears?

"Come on, you guys," I urge them. "Don't you want the 4A *Gazette* to win the student newspaper contest?"

I already know the answer. Of course Aiden and Emma want to win that newspaper contest. We all do. The winning class gets a visit from Scoop Schaeffer. He's a real reporter who has won all sorts of awards. It would be exciting to have him visit Class 4A. Especially for me, because as the editor of our class newspaper, I would be Scoop's personal host. I'd even get to have lunch with him.

But if we're going to win that visit from Scoop, we're going to have to come up with an amazing front-page story. One that no other class has thought of. A story that will grab readers and make them want to read.

A real scoop.

Hey, I wonder if that's how Scoop Schaeffer got his name.

"Of course I want to win," Aiden insists. "That's why I think we need to have the flag football story on the front page. Think about it—we'll get the inside story on what it takes to make a championship team. I could interview myself."

"Interview yourself?" I shake my head. "No way."

"Sports stories go on the *back* page," Emma argues. "But a dance recital could be front-page news."

"Stop fighting," I plead with them. "Everyone will get an article in the paper."

"But not on the *front page*," Emma points out. "And that's the page everyone sees, even if they don't read the whole paper."

"Speaking of dancing," Olivia interrupts. "Do you know how you make a tissue dance?"

"How?" Emma wonders.

"Put a little boogie in it!" Olivia starts laughing at her own joke.

I shoot my twin a grateful look. I'm glad she was able to stop Aiden and Emma from arguing—if only for a second. "That's a funny one," I tell her.

"Do newspapers have joke pages?" Olivia asks.

I shake my head. "Not usually. But they do have comic strips."

"I could write a comic strip," Olivia says. "I just can't *draw* it."

My sister and I both stare at Tony.

"What?" he asks, even though he knows what we're thinking.

Tony draws all the time. You should see his math notebook. It's filled with drawings. Not much math. But *lots* of drawings.

"Are you serious?" he asks me. "You want me to work with *Olivia*?"

"What's wrong with that?" Olivia demands.

"You're never nice to me," Tony reminds her.

"I am sometimes," Olivia insists.

"Name twice," Tony says.

"Please, Tony," I urge. "You're the best artist in our class. Maybe in the whole fourth grade."

Emma scowls at that. Probably because she's always bragging about how she might be an artist when she grows up. Or an actress. Or a singer. Or a dancer.

"You could be the best artist in the whole school," Olivia tells Tony.

Okay, now my sister's going a little over-board.

Tony stares at Olivia. I think he's trying to figure out if she's teasing him or not.

I don't blame him. My sister is a champion teaser.

Tony looks from Olivia to me, and back again. "Fine," he tells Olivia. "I'll work with you. Just be nice, okay?"

"I promise," Olivia agrees.

"Great!" Emma exclaims. "You can put

their comic strip on the page before Aiden's football story."

*Ugh.*

I look at my teacher. She's sitting at her desk, happily knitting something that looks like a giant sweater, except it has four armholes.

She could be knitting a sweater for a really big dog.

Or a horse.

Or some four-armed alien from outer space. You never know with Ms. Frogbottom.

"What do you think?" I ask, hoping she'll make the decision for me.

"You're the editor," Ms. Frogbottom replies. "It's up to you."

That's not what I wanted to hear. No matter what I say now, Aiden or Emma will be mad at me.

Actually, they're *both* going to be mad at me. "I don't think either of your stories should go on the front page," I tell them.

"I wish Ms. Frogbottom had made me editor," Emma complains.

"You mean made *me* editor," Aiden argues.

*Oh brother.* If we don't win this student newspaper contest, I just know that Aiden and Emma are going to blame me.

I'll probably blame me too.

Unless . . .

I look over at Sofia. She's been sitting at her desk, quietly doing a crossword puzzle. Sofia is the class brain. Maybe she can use her smarts to come up with a great story idea. "Do you have an article you want to write?" I ask her.

"Actually, I have a strong story idea," she says.

*Awesome.*

"I want to cover the science fair," she

continues. "The fifth grade has been building dinosaur models with Popsicle sticks."

*Awesome. Not.*

"That's your great story idea? Model dinosaurs?"

"What do you want her to do, *Liver*?" Olivia asks me. "Find a real dinosaur?"

"Don't call me 'Liver,'" I tell her.

Olivia laughs. "Can't you take a joke?"

See what I mean about my sister being a champion teaser?

"Scientists believe that birds are in the same family as dinosaurs," Sofia tells us. "I could write about ornithology. . . ."

"Orange what?" I ask her.

"*Ornithology*," Sofia repeats. "An eleven-letter word that means 'the study of birds.'

It was the answer to a clue in last week's crossword puzzle."

It's one thing to learn new words when Ms. Frogbottom puts them on the board as our Word of the Day. But Sofia memorizes vocabulary words just for fun. Of course, it's easy for her. She has a photographic memory. Everything she reads, she remembers.

Unfortunately, Sofia's ability to memorize big words doesn't help me right now. "I wasn't talking about birds," I tell her. "I meant a huge dinosaur. Like in a museum. How cool would it be if we found one that was still alive?"

"It would be terrible," Tony argues. "A dinosaur could eat us."

"Only if it was a carnivore," Sofia corrects him. "Herbivores don't eat meat."

"Don't worry," I assure Tony. "It's not like there's a dinosaur out there terrorizing our town."

"Not *this* town," Ms. Frogbottom chimes in. "But there is a place that might have what you're looking for. . . ." She reaches into her backpack and pulls out a giant map.

There's no way the map should fit into her pack, but somehow it does.

Her taking the map out can mean only

one thing. We're going on one of Ms. Frog-bottom's field trips.

"Here we go again," Olivia whispers.

"But *where*?" Aiden wonders.

"I hope it's someplace fancy." Emma rubs lip balm across her lips.

Sofia grabs her tablet. She won't go anywhere without it.

"Have I mentioned how afraid I am of Ms. Frogbottom's field trips?" Tony asks nervously. "Something bad always happens. Remember when the Magic Map took us to Egypt? We met that mummy who wanted to trap us forever in his tomb of doom."

Of course I remember. You don't forget something like that.

"Don't worry, Tony," I tell him. "No

matter where we go, we won't be there forever. We're always back from field trips by dismissal."

Ms. Frogbottom points to a spot on the other side of the Atlantic Ocean.

Suddenly a white light flashes all around us. My body feels weightless, and I think my feet have just left the ground.

It's like I'm flying in space. And then . . .

## WE'RE HERE.

Wherever *here* is. All I know is that we're not in our classroom at Left Turn Alleyway Elementary anymore. Instead I'm standing on a big lawn at the edge of a town, staring out at a humongous dark lake.

"Look!" Emma exclaims suddenly. "A unicorn! I think we're in a magical fairy-land!"

*Unicorn?* My news-editor brain starts to buzz. If we were to meet a real-life unicorn, it would be the biggest story any classroom newspaper has ever run. I turn excitedly to see where Emma is pointing and—

*Ugh.* My news-editor-brain buzz disappears.

Emma is pointing to a *flag* with a unicorn on it. It's flying in front of a large, old, stone building across the road from the lake. Above the unicorn flag is another flag—blue with a big white *X* on it.

Sofia is staring at her tablet. She scrolls for a few seconds, and then shakes her head. "Sorry, Emma. This isn't a magical fairyland. It's a country called Scotland. The unicorn is their national animal. That blue-and-white flag is the *official* flag of Scotland."

"Yes, Sofia!" Ms. Frogbottom cheers. "We are in Scotland. And what a field trip this will be! Today we're going to use our senses to experience everything Scotland has to offer. We're going to try traditional Scottish food, visit a castle, and hopefully take a boat ride on the lake. "

"You mean on the *loch*," Sofia says.

"Yes, I suppose I do," Ms. Frogbottom replies with a laugh.

"Did you guys hear the song about the woman who kept switching the locks on her front door?" Olivia asks us.

"Yeah," I answer. "The song had a lot of *key changes*."

"I love that joke," my sister says, laughing.

"It's not that kind of lock," Sofia explains. "You spell it *L-O-C-H*. That's the Scottish word for 'lake.'"

Sometimes Sofia has no sense of humor.

*Bang. Bang. Bang.*

*Tap. Tap. Tap.*

And speaking of music . . . there's some coming from down the block. A guy with a drum set and a woman with a violin have just set up on the sidewalk across the street. A group of women in yellow dresses are dancing as the musicians play.

*Bang. Bang. Bang.*

*Tap. Tap. Tap.*

Each of the women is kicking one of her legs out in front of her and bending her back leg. As they kick and bend, they tap their heels and toes to the beat.

A group of tourists is gathering around, watching.

"Oh, how wonderful!" Ms. Frogbottom exclaims. "Scottish step dancers."

"I've never seen dancing like this," Olivia says.

"It's a traditional Scottish folk dance," Ms. Frogbottom tells her.

"It doesn't seem hard," Emma says. "We do much more difficult choreography in my dance class."

Emma kicks one leg out in front and taps her heel. Then she bends her other leg and taps her toe. Kick. Bend. Kick. Be—

*Whoops!* Emma's feet slip out from

under her. She lands on her rear end with a *thud*.

Aiden laughs. "That's gonna be some dance recital," he whispers to me.

Emma sticks her tongue out at him.

"Don't feel bad, Emma," Ms. Frogbottom tells her. "It can take years to learn to step dance."

As the dancers finish, Ms. Frogbottom and my classmates applaud. But I'm busy watching three people who are standing next to a van parked by the water.

At first I'm thinking it's just a bunch of friends having a picnic. Then I see they're setting up a big video camera with its own stand. A woman is holding a microphone on a long stick.

"They're making a movie!" Emma squeals. Then she fluffs her hair and waves her arms in the air. "This could be my big break. Yoo-hoo! Director!"

Suddenly some guy wearing rubber boots comes racing from the old stone building across the road. He's shouting angrily at the people near the van. "Get outta here, ye nasty news folk!"

*News* folk?

That's not a movie crew. It's a TV news crew. They must be working on a story. Now *I'm* the one who's excited.

"Why is a news crew here?" I ask the man.

The angry man runs his hand through the small patch of white in the middle of his dark hair, and grumbles.

"Oliver." Ms. Frogbottom gives me a stern look. "Don't you think you should introduce yourself before you start asking questions?"

"Sorry," I apologize. "Hi. I'm Oliver. Why is a news crew here?"

"Every time they park there, they block the view of the loch from my inn," the man replies, not answering my question. He points to the big picture window at the front of the stone building. "It's not good for business."

I want to point out to Ms. Frogbottom that this man did not introduce himself to *me*, but I don't think she'd like that. Besides, I have something more important on my mind than this guy's name.

"*Every time?*" I repeat. "Why do they keep coming back?"

"No good reason," the man answers. "Because I assure you that Nessie isn't going to show up with that camera around. He doesn't want his picture taken." The man sighs. "I gotta go back to my kitchen and get cooking."

Then he leaves. Just like that. He doesn't even say good-bye. All we hear is the *clip-clop, clip-clop* of his heavy rain boots as he trudges back to his inn.

"I wonder who Nessie is," I say as he leaves.

"Maybe he's a famous Scottish movie star?" Emma asks excitedly. "I could interview him. That would get my story on the front page. Wouldn't it, Oliver?"

"Nessie could be a famous athlete," Aiden counters. "An interview with him would be front-page news. Right, Oliver?"

"Nessie isn't a movie star or a sports star," Sofia says as she looks at something on her tablet. "He's a monster."

"A m-m-monster?" Tony stammers nervously. "Does it live in that water? Like a sea monster?"

"Well, more like a *lake* monster. 'Nessie' is a nickname for the Loch Ness Monster," Sofia continues, ignoring how scared Tony seems. "And according to this article, he's possibly an ancient dinosaur—who is still alive and roaming the loch."

*A dinosaur!* So that's what Ms. Frogbottom meant about taking us to a place that had what we were looking for. My brain is so excited, it feels like it might pop out of my skull!

"Nessie's also a real troublemaker," Sofia continues. "Apparently he captures anything or anyone who threatens him, and then eats them!"

"E-e-eats them?" Tony's voice is shaking so badly that I can barely make out what he's saying. "That's terrible."

"You're not kidding," Aiden agrees. "Eating people is disgusting. And I'm someone who'll eat just about anything."

My friends are standing around, talking about the article Sofia is reading. But I don't want to hear what some article says. I want to see this monster up close.

Okay, maybe not up close. Because

## FROGBOTTOM FACTS

★ Scotland is a country that is part of the United Kingdom, along with England, Northern Ireland, and Wales.
★ There are more than thirty thousand freshwater lochs (or lakes) in Scotland.
★ "Loch Ness" is the name of a freshwater lake located in the Scottish Highlands a few miles from the city of Inverness.

I don't want to be eaten. I just want to be close enough to catch a glimpse of him. I can't just stand here when there's a news story happening.

I have to find out why those reporters think there's a monster in that lake.

# 3

I HAVE SO MANY QUESTIONS RIGHT NOW. And like any other newsman, I have to go where the answers are. Which, in this case, is down by that lake.

But I'm still a *kid* newsman. So I need permission to go pretty much anywhere.

"Can we get a little closer to the lake?" I ask Ms. Frogbottom.

"I was just going to suggest that," our teacher replies. "I want you all to see the wildlife around here. There are salmon and eel in the water. If we're really lucky, we might see pawprints in the mud at the water's edge. Possibly from a herd of red deer or a wild hare."

I don't know why Ms. Frogbottom sounds so excited. The water in that lake is so dark, I doubt we'd be able to see any fish swimming below the surface. And I can look for animal pawprints in my backyard. We have deer and rabbits there, too.

## FROGBOTTOM FACTS

★ There is more water in Loch Ness than in all the lakes of England and Wales combined.
★ Loch Ness is so dark because the heavy rains wash particles of decaying plants from the surrounding hills into the water.

I'm more interested in spotting something I can't find at home.

*I want to see the Loch Ness Monster.*

Because an article about a monster sighting is something you wouldn't find in any other classroom newspaper. That would be the kind of scoop that could really get people reading—not to mention win our class a visit from Scoop Schaeffer!

"Is it okay if I talk to the reporters instead?" I ask Ms. Frogbottom.

Ms. Frogbottom smiles. "I'm so glad you've taken an interest in journalism, Oliver," she tells me. "*Of course* you can talk to them. Just be careful walking on the pebbles. They can be slippery."

"Thanks!" I run off before she can change her mind.

"Hi. I'm Oliver," I say, to introduce myself as I get close to the van.

"Now's not really a good time, kid," a tall man with red hair tells me. He doesn't even look in my direction.

"I'm not a *kid*," I insist.

The tall guy rolls his eyes.

"Well, I mean I *am* a kid," I admit. "But I'm also a news guy, like you. In fact, I'm an *editor*."

"An editor. Isn't that cute?" a woman in a pink sweater says with a giggle. She's not taking me seriously. But that won't stop me. I *will* get this story for the *4A Gazette*.

"Are you looking for the Loch Ness Monster?" I ask.

"What do you know about that?" the guy with red hair asks angrily.

"Take it easy, Finn," the woman holding

the microphone urges. "It's not like some lad's gonna scoop us."

*Ha! That's what she thinks.*

"Okay, Amelia." The woman with the microphone turns her attention to the lady in the pink sweater. "Let's run a sound check."

"Right, Millie," Amelia says. "Test. One, two."

"Why do you think the monster is in *this* loch?" I ask them.

"Because this water is called 'Loch Ness.' And he's the *Loch Ness Monster,*" Finn replies gruffly.

That makes sense.

"The guy from the inn says you've been here before," I continue. "Does

★ 41 ★

that mean you've already spotted the monster?"

"You've been talking to Mr. Dreich?" Amelia is taking me a little more seriously now.

"Yes," I say. "He's a very good source. *We* newspeople need good sources for our stories."

"If you've been talking to Mr. Dreich, then you know that a lot of mysterious

things have been happening around here lately," Millie tells me.

"Like what?" I wonder.

"You sure you want us to tell you, laddie?" Amelia asks. "Because you won't want to be anywhere near this loch after we do."

"I'm sure."

"Well, it all started last week, on a calm, quiet morning," Amelia tells me. "There wasn't a drop of wind. Yet a small fishing boat began to toss back and forth on the water—and then it capsized. Just flipped right over. The fisherman nearly drowned."

"Maybe he stood up in the boat," I suggest. "That could have made it tip."

"We spoke to the fisherman," Amelia assures me. "He wasn't standing."

"It gets worse," Finn adds. "Animals that live by the loch have been disappearing. Someone—or some*thing*—has been grabbing deer in the dark of night and dragging them into the loch. We know because the hoofprints are all leading into the water."

"Maybe the deer wanted a drink," I suggest.

"Could be," Finn agrees. "Except there are no hoofprints leading *away* from the loch. Which means the deer went in but never came out."

*Okay, that's a little creepy.*

I look over at my class. They're studying animal prints in the mud. I wonder if

they've noticed that the deer prints only seem to be going in one direction.

Probably not. Tony looks pretty happy. If he'd figured out something like that, he'd be freaking out.

"And then there are the noises," Millie adds.

"The noises?" I reply, trying really hard not to sound nervous.

"The local folk have been hearing them in the middle of the night, when the sky is at its darkest," Millie tells me. "Deep, angry honking noises. Almost like a huge flock of geese, all honking at the same time. Only, there are no birds in the sky. And the noise seems to be coming from *inside* the water, not over it."

*I have to admit that's kinda unusual. But still . . .*

"You're not *sure* it's a monster, are you?" I ask. "I mean, you have no *real* proof."

"You want proof?" Millie reaches into her pocket and shows me a blurry black-and-white photograph of what looks like a giant dinosaur-lizard head popping out of the water.

"Whoa!" I exclaim. "That picture was taken here?"

Millie nods.

"Laddie, you'd better get away from Loch Ness," Finn warns me.

"Because of the monster?"

"Nah," Finn replies. "*You're* more likely to be gotten by a kelpie."

"A what?"

"You've never heard of a kelpie?" Finn sounds surprised.

I shake my head.

"You'd better hope you never meet one," he says. "They're more dangerous than Nessie would ever be—at least for you."

Maybe it's the way the sky has darkened. Or maybe it's the way the fog has come up around Loch Ness, making the air so gray and thick that I can barely see the hills around the lake. But something about what Finn is saying makes me really nervous.

"Because kelpies *eat* children," Finn continues.

"They trick kids into coming close, and

then they capture them and eat them for breakfast," Millie adds.

"Or lunch, or dinner." Finn laughs.

"Trick them?" I ask, trying to act like a real reporter, even though there are now a flock of nervous butterflies flying around in my stomach. "How?"

"Shape-shifting," Millie replies mysteriously.

"What's that?" I ask.

Millie opens her mouth to answer, but whatever she's saying is drowned out by a sudden, huge clap of thunder.

The sound makes me jump six feet in the air. Which is odd, because I'm not usually scared of thunder. Loch Ness is making me really jumpy.

*Whoosh!*

In a flash the rain starts pouring down on us.

"Quick—get the equipment back into the van!" Finn shouts.

These guys aren't going to answer any more questions right now. They're too busy hurrying to get their cameras and microphones out of the rain.

"Come along, Oliver," Ms. Frogbottom calls to me. "We're going into the inn."

I turn away from the news crew and race to catch up to my class.

But this conversation isn't over. Not by a long shot.

"SHAPE-SHIFTING?" OLIVIA REPEATS a few minutes later as she takes off her shoes and leaves them to dry near the old stone fireplace in the lobby of Mr. Dreich's inn.

"Uh-huh," I reply, placing my shoes next to my sister's.

"What does that even mean?" Olivia wonders.

I shrug. "We didn't get that far. I think they were just trying to scare me off so

I wouldn't scoop them on their big Loch
Ness Monster story."

Sofia pulls her tablet out from under
her shirt, where she'd been trying to keep
it dry, and she starts scrolling around.
"'Kelpies are creatures that switch back
and forth between being horses and
humans,'" she reads. "The only thing that

gives them away is that when they're in human form, they don't have feet."

"F-f-footless m-m-monsters?" Tony stammers nervously. "That means they won't make foot*steps* when they walk. You won't hear them sneaking up behind you."

"You didn't let me finish. And this part is *really* interesting," Sofia tells Tony. "Kelpies don't have feet, but they do have hooves. Even when they're in human form."

*A person with horse feet.* That would look really strange. But it would also make kelpies pretty easy to spot when they're in human form.

"They could wear shoes over their hooves," Tony points out. "That would disguise them."

*Hmmm.* I didn't think of that.

"Very good, Tony," Ms. Frogbottom says. "I like the way you used logic there."

Usually Tony would be smiling proudly at Ms. Frogbottom's compliment. But today he's too nervous to be proud. I can tell because he's chewing at the stringy skin around his fingernails.

"Do you know what it means when you find a horseshoe?" Olivia asks him.

"What?" Tony replies.

"Some horse is walking around in his socks," Olivia says with a laugh.

"Not funny." Tony goes back to chewing his fingers.

"I'm with Tony," I say.

Olivia looks at me in surprise. "Don't tell me you're afraid too, Liver. Or should I call you *Chicken Liver*?"

*Ugh.* There she goes again.

"I just meant it wasn't a funny joke," I insist. Which isn't exactly true. I'm actually a little scared of being eaten by a shape-shifting horse-human.

Wouldn't *you* be?

"Does that webpage say anything about *how* kelpies catch kids?" I ask Sofia.

She nods. "They act like gentle horses and trick kids into climbing onto their backs. Once the kid is up there, the kelpie gallops into the water, making sure the kid drowns. Then the kelpie eats him."

"So here in Scotland there's a Loch Ness Monster that attacks and eats people who make him angry," Tony says. "And there are also kelpies that eat kids. Aren't any Scottish monsters vegetarians?"

"I've never heard of any herbivore monsters," Sofia says. "I don't think one would be scary if all it ate were plants. And a monster wouldn't be a monster if it weren't scary."

"She's got a point," Emma agrees.

"I'm not going near any horses while we're here," Tony vows. "There's no way I'm gonna be a kelpie lunch!"

"Speaking of lunch," Aiden says, "I wonder what kind of food they serve in Scotland. I'm hungry."

Aiden is *always* hungry. "Nothing can kill *your* appetite," I tell him.

Tony shoots me a look.

Okay, maybe "kill" wasn't the best word to use, considering.

Ms. Frogbottom pulls a pink-and-white feathered hat out of her backpack. "I don't think it's ever too early for high tea," she tells us as she places the huge hat on her head.

"I don't want *tea*," Aiden complains. "I want food."

"Don't worry," Ms. Frogbottom assures him. "There's plenty to eat at a Scottish high tea."

We follow Ms. Frogbottom into the next room, where a long wooden table has been set with china plates and a fancy tablecloth.

"Oh, look at this lovely lace!" Ms. Frogbottom exclaims as she gently runs her hand over the tablecloth. "I'll bet that was made by hand on a loom. The finest Scottish lace usually is."

My teacher picks up one of the plates and looks at the flowery pattern around the edges. "Scottish bone china is so unique," she remarks.

"*Bone* china?" Tony repeats nervously. "I don't like the sound of that. Is it made of real bones?"

Ms. Frogbottom smiles at him. "Actually, yes. The finest bone china has ashes from cows and sheep in its clay."

Tony frowns. That wasn't the answer he was hoping for.

I don't usually go to such swanky places. I hope I don't break one of those plates, or spill something onto the tablecloth.

The dining room smells really good. Like a combination of meat frying and cake baking. Now I'm hungry too.

"We'll start today's high tea with blood pudding," Mr. Dreich says as he comes out of the kitchen carrying a big tray.

"*Blood* pudding?" Tony asks, his voice scaling up nervously. "What about chocolate or vanilla? I'd even eat tapioca."

"*Blood,*" Mr. Dreich repeats. He places a giant sausage in front of each of us.

"This isn't pudding," I tell him. "Pudding is soft and creamy."

"We call that custard here, laddie," Mr. Dreich replies. "Blood pudding is made of meat and pig's blood."

"I'll pass," Tony says.

"At least try the rumbledethumps," Mr. Dreich urges, placing some sort of fried dish on his plate. "It's my special recipe—potatoes, turnips, cabbage, and cheese."

"No blood?" Tony asks nervously.

"Not a bit," Mr. Dreich assures him as he serves the rest of us our blood pudding and rumbledethumps.

Aiden takes a big bite of his blood pudding. "You're making a mistake, Tony," he says. "This sausage is delicious."

"Scary lake monsters, shape-shifting kid-eaters, plates made with bones, and sausages made of blood?" Tony's voice is shaky. "I'm not liking it here."

"Scotland is lovely," Mr. Dreich insists.

"The weather isn't," Olivia says. "That rain came out of nowhere."

"We wouldn't be in Scotland if we didn't see some rain," Ms. Frogbottom says, laughing. "One minute there's a storm, and the next the sun is shining."

"Which gives us beautiful rainbows," Mr. Dreich adds.

"I love rainbows," Emma says. "I hope we see one when we visit that castle."

"Oh, so you will be visiting Urquhart Castle?" Mr. Dreich asks us.

Ms. Frogbottom nods. "I think it's important to learn the history of the places you visit, don't you?"

"Indeed," Mr. Dreich agrees. "That castle's been around for nearly eight hundred years, so there's plenty of history in those stone walls. Think of all the nobles who slept in that great chamber, and all the enemies who spent their last minutes in that prison cell."

Tony gulps. "*Last* minutes?"

"And of course there are the wonderful views of the loch," Mr. Dreich continues. "There have been quite a few Nessie sightings from up there."

Hmmm. Now, that sounds interesting.

"I'm going to get your dessert," Mr. Dreich tells us. "I've baked fresh fruit tarts. Since you kids are taking your meals at my inn while you're in Scotland, it's my job to fatten you up."

Then he heads into his kitchen, his heavy rain boots making a *clip-clop* noise on the wood floors of the inn.

"Fat. Just the way the kelpies like us," Olivia tells Tony.

Tony bites harder at his fingers. A drop of red pops up on his thumb. I guess he's having blood for lunch, after all. His *own* blood.

"Why is that innkeeper wearing rain boots inside?" Emma wonders.

"His name is 'Mr. Dreich,'" I tell her. "The news guys told me."

"Okay. Why is *Mr. Dreich* wearing his boots inside?" Emma corrects herself.

"I don't care if he's wearing *bunny slippers*," Aiden replies. "He baked us fruit tarts. Bring on the sweets."

"I wish *I* had rubber boots," I say. "The stones by the loch are going to be really muddy and slippery when the rain stops."

"You're not going back there, are you?" Tony asks nervously.

"I sure am," I insist. "I'm not going to let that news crew scoop me."

"Nessie's liable to scoop you—right into the lake," Tony warns me. "Monsters are called monsters for a reason."

Tony doesn't understand. Sometimes a reporter has to risk encountering monsters in order to get a big story.

"I don't think you have to worry about the Loch Ness Monster, Tony," Sofia tells him. "He doesn't really exist."

Tony stops biting his fingers.

"Those reporters wouldn't be here waiting for him if he were made up," I point out to Sofia. "They even have an old picture of him. I saw it."

"The best-known picture of Nessie was a

fake," Sofia argues. "Just a wooden dummy glued to a toy submarine. *There's no such thing as the Loch Ness Monster.*"

"NAY!" Mr. Dreich exclaims as he walks back into the room. "You're wrong, lassie!" He slams the dessert platter onto the table so hard, the tarts bounce off the tray. Aiden catches one in midair and takes a big bite.

"This is delicious," he says between chews. Little pieces of fruit tart fly out of his mouth as he talks.

"The famous photo of Nessie wasn't real," Sofia insists, ignoring Aiden.

"Maybe that picture was a fake, but Nessie isn't," Mr. Dreich tells her. "People have been spotting him since before there were cameras. Saint Columba saw a monster in Loch Ness nearly fifteen hundred years ago. Dr. Mackenzie saw Nessie churning up the waters in the 1800s."

"But—" Sofia begins

"Nessie is very real," Mr. Dreich says, cutting her off. "Dangerous, too. Especially when he thinks someone is after him. Like those reporters."

"They're not *after* Nessie," I insist. "They just want a story."

"Once it gets out that Nessie's been spotted again, this place will be filled with people who want to catch him and put him on display . . . or *worse*," Mr. Dreich says in a worrisome voice.

*Hmmm.* I hadn't thought of that.

"That's going to put folks in danger," he

★ **66** ★

continues. "Because the Loch Ness Monster will do *anything* to keep from getting caught."

"I don't like the sound of that," Tony says, biting even harder at his fingers.

Now we all seem a little scared. We're just sitting there, staring at Ms. Frogbottom, hoping our teacher will tell us that everything will be okay.

But Ms. Frogbottom doesn't say a word.

And somehow that makes everything scarier.

## FROGBOTTOM FACTS

★ The custom of Scottish high tea started in the 1600s. It was a meal served to workmen at the end of the day, usually around five o'clock in the afternoon.

★ High tea got its name because the meal was eaten while sitting at a high table, as opposed to sitting on comfortable sofas and chairs.

# 5

"I CAN'T BELIEVE WE'RE GOING TO VISIT a real castle!" Emma exclaims excitedly as we walk up the hill to Urquhart Castle. "Will we get to see a princess, Ms. Frogbottom?"

Our teacher shakes her head. "Sorry, Emma. No one has lived at Urquhart Castle since the 1600s."

We cross over a wooden bridge, taking care not to slip on the wet wood beneath our

feet. On one side of us, I can see Loch Ness. On the other I see green hills and trees. Oh, and sheep. Lots and lots of sheep.

"Look up there!" exclaims Ms. Frogbottom, pointing overhead. "That's a golden eagle! Isn't it majestic?"

## FROGBOTTOM FACTS

★ Scotland has more sheep than people.
★ There are almost fifteen thousand sheep farms in Scotland.

My teacher pulls a small notebook and a pencil from her backpack. "Golden eagle," she says as she writes in her book. "I can't wait to tell the members of my bird-watching group that I spotted one of those."

We walk a little farther, until Ms. Frogbottom stops and points to some broken stone walls that look like they were once a part of a building but aren't anymore.

"Here we are!" she announces excitedly.

Urquhart Castle doesn't look like any castle I've ever seen in the movies. There are a few places that seem like they were once buildings, but mostly all I see are piles of rocks, with signs telling us what *used* to be here.

"This is it?" Emma sounds really bummed.

"Yes!" Ms. Frogbottom exclaims. "Isn't it marvelous?"

"Not really," Emma says. "Everything looks like it was blown up."

"Exactly," Ms. Frogbottom replies. "The last army to live here blew up parts of the castle before they left. They wanted to make sure their enemies wouldn't be able to use it."

"There were armies here?" Aiden asks.

"Oh yes," Ms. Frogbottom says. "Can't you just picture the soldiers fighting with their swords, guns, and crossbows on this hill? Imagine the excitement of the MacDonald clan when they stormed the castle back in 1545. They were able to steal almost nine thousand animals, twenty guns, and three boats. Not to mention beds, sheets, chairs, doors—"

"Doors?" Aiden asks. "Why would anybody want to take doors?"

"They were probably beautifully carved and decorated," Sofia suggests. "It sounds like the MacDonald clan took anything of value from Urquhart Castle."

"What's that building?" Olivia points to a tower made of stacked stones, with small holes that look like they were once windows.

"Grant Tower," Ms. Frogbottom replies. "It's named for the Grant family, who built the building in the 1500s and . . ."

Ms. Frogbottom is telling us all sorts of

stuff about the tower, but I'm not listening. I'm just thinking about how badly I want to be back at the edge of Loch Ness, waiting with that news crew for Nessie to appear.

I know that could be dangerous. But "Danger" is a news kid's middle name.

Okay, my middle name is Zachary, but you know what I mean.

"You can see most of Loch Ness from the top of the tower," Ms. Frogbottom continues, pointing straight up.

Wait a minute! That's it!

Mr. Dreich said people had reported seeing the Loch Ness Monster from the castle. If I got a glimpse of him from up there, I wouldn't be in any danger. It's the perfect plan!

"Let's go up!" I cheer.

Tony gives me a look. "Didn't you hear Ms. Frogbottom? That tower's almost forty feet high!"

I didn't hear her say that. But I think it's great.

"Think of what we could see from up there!" I don't say anything about possibly spotting the Loch Ness Monster. There's no sense in freaking Tony out again. But seeing the monster is definitely what I'm imagining.

Actually, I'm imagining what will happen after I write my Loch Ness Monster newspaper story. I might get a medal for it. I bet Scoop Schaeffer would be really impressed to meet a news kid with a medal.

I wonder if they throw parades for newspaper editors.

"There's no way I'm going up there," Tony says nervously.

"Maybe we should look at something else," Aiden suggests. "Didn't Mr. Dreich say there was a prison here? That could be cool."

"No!" I shout suddenly. "Why are we letting Tony ruin everything?"

"Oliver!" Ms. Frogbottom sounds really upset with me. "That's no way to speak about your friend. Apologize to Tony immediately."

"I'm sorry you're afraid of heights," I say.

"Try again," Ms. Frogbottom orders sternly.

"I'm sorry, Tony. I shouldn't have said you were ruining everything."

"I didn't mean to ruin *anything*," Tony insists.

Now the other kids are looking at me like *I'm* a monster. And not the kind of monster that belongs on the front page of the *4A Gazette*.

"Perhaps we should go look at where

the stables once stood," Ms. Frogbottom suggests. "Come along."

We follow behind her.

"Scottish Highland horses had to be especially strong," Ms. Frogbottom tells us. "When lords and ladies traveled, the horses pulled all their belongings up and down the hills. And . . . *oh my!*"

Our teacher stops suddenly and stares at a bird by some nearby trees. "There's a capercaillie, one of the rarest birds in this area. I have to get a better look. I'll just go over by those pine trees while you all explore the stables." And with that, she hurries off into the trees.

I don't exactly know what Ms. Frogbottom wants us to explore. All I see are some rocks that look like they might have been at the bottom of a building at one time. You wouldn't even know what had been here if there wasn't a sign that said THE STABLES.

"Look!" Emma exclaims suddenly. She points toward the rocks.

A real horse has emerged from behind the pile of stones. It's black with a small patch of white fur on the top of its head.

"That's strange," Sofia replies, studying her tablet. "There haven't been any horses in the Urquhart Castle stables for hundreds of years."

"Well, there's one here now," Emma tells her. "It's beautiful! Look at that shiny fur."

"That horse isn't supposed to be here," Sofia says. "I wonder where it came from."

"Who cares?" Emma declares. "It's pretty. And it seems so gentle." She starts walking toward the horse.

"Don't!" Tony exclaims.

"Quiet," Emma warns. "You'll scare it off."

"If that's a kelpie, I *want* to scare it off," Tony tells her.

"Tony," Sofia says calmly. "You don't really believe all that shape-shifting stuff, do you?"

"Yeah," Aiden agrees. "This is just a horse."

Suddenly there's a flash of lightning against the gray sky. A few seconds later the thunder booms.

The horse runs off in fright just as Ms. Frogbottom hurries toward us.

"We should head back . . . ," she begins, reaching into her backpack.

*No. No. No! Please don't pull out the Magic Map*, I pray silently. I don't want to go back to school until I see that monster and get my medal—I mean my *story*.

". . . to the inn," Ms. Frogbottom finishes as she fishes umbrellas out of her pack and hands them to us.

*Yes. Yes. Yes!* We may have a chance to spot the Loch Ness Monster after all.

## 6

**"Have you spotted Nessie yet?" I ask** Finn a little while later. The rain has let up and the fog has cleared. Finn, Amelia, and Millie are back on the rocky shore of Loch Ness with their news reporting equipment all set up and ready to go.

"Please, laddie," Finn says. "Let us do our jobs."

Finn is still trying to get rid of me. But at least this time he said "please."

"Do you have the video camera ready?" Amelia asks Finn.

"Oh yeah," Finn assures her. "If Nessie's out there, we'll get our shot."

I wish I had a camera with me. Newspaper articles are so much better with photos.

But Ms. Frogbottom has a strict rule. No taking photos when we go on our field trips. She says she wants us to experience everything firsthand, through our senses. Not through a camera lens.

"Hey, Oliver? You want to play soccer?" Aiden calls out.

My classmates are kicking a ball around on the wet grass a few feet from the news van. They're keeping busy as we all wait for Ms. Frogbottom to come back from the old inn across the road. She went there to find Mr. Dreich and get us a snack. Because Aiden is hungry—*again*.

While our teacher is at the inn, we're supposed to stay together and not leave the area. Which we won't. None of us would disobey Ms. Frogbottom. There's nothing worse than having to have a "talk" with her about "how disappointed" she is in our behavior. Those talks are awful.

"In Scotland it's called 'football,' not 'soccer,'" Sofia corrects Aiden. She kicks the ball—hard. It soars across the grass at top speed.

"Whoa!" Aiden compliments Sofia. "You kick like Rose Reilly—and she was one of Scotland's greatest soccer players."

"Thanks!" Sofia replies with a grin.

"Oliver, are you gonna play with us or what?" Olivia demands.

My sister wants me to play soccer *now*? When at any minute the Loch Ness Monster could pop out of that lake?

*Or not.*

Loch Ness is completely still. If there's a monster in there, he's not moving.

Maybe I should just go kick the ball around a bit. My classmates seem like they're having fun and—

"Look at that!" I shout out suddenly. "Something's happening in the loch!"

Suddenly the news crew leaps into action. Amelia, Millie, and Finn are all shouting at once and pointing toward the middle of the lake. Waves are starting to churn, even though there's no wind blowing.

Whatever is making those waves is definitely *in* Loch Ness.

I'm getting excited. My nose for news is telling me that something big is about to go down.

And I'm not the only one who thinks so. My classmates are racing over to the water's edge. They want to take a closer look at what's going on too.

"Check it out!" Aiden exclaims.

"I don't like this," Tony adds nervously. "Not one bit."

"Fascinating," Sofia mumbles as she stares up into the sky. A whole flock of birds has taken off from the trees and flown away from the lake. "It's too bad Ms. Frogbottom had to go find Mr. Dreich. She would have loved seeing all those birds."

"WHOA!" Finn's eyes look like they're going to burst from his head.

I don't blame him. Three big, slimy humps are popping out of the water. That could be the back of—

"Nessie!" Amelia exclaims.

*Exactly what I was thinking.*

"We're going out there!" Finn races

over to the news van. "Help me with the rowboat, Millie."

He doesn't have to ask her twice. Millie hurries over. Together she and Finn pull out a small wooden boat.

"Out of the way, kids," Millie says as she and Finn push the boat out onto the water. "We've got a news story to go after."

So do I. I really want to get into that boat and go out on Loch Ness. It's not like Ms. Frogbottom said I couldn't do that. In fact, I distinctly remember her saying we were going to take a boat ride today.

But I bet she didn't mean we should get into a boat without her.

Besides, Ms. Frogbottom told our class to stay together while she went across the street. And there isn't enough room in that boat for all of us.

So I'm stuck on the shore watching with everyone else as Millie climbs into the rowboat and sits between the oars. Finn and Amelia climb in too. Then they row out into the loch.

"I can't believe they went out in a rowboat without life jackets," Tony says.

"Do you really think a life jacket would protect them from an angry, vicious, dinosaur-size monster?" I ask Tony.

Tony shrugs. "It couldn't hurt." He looks out at the choppy dark waters of Loch Ness. "Those guys are idiots."

"No, they're not," I argue. "They're reporters. Sheesh, Tony."

Tony frowns. I think I may have hurt his feelings.

But he isn't even *trying* to understand how important getting this story is to me. And that hurts *my* feelings.

"Look at that water blow!" Olivia exclaims. "It's like a hurricane."

She's not kidding. The waves are shooting into the air, with their white-caps bumping wildly into one another as they come crashing down. The roar of the waves is so loud, I can barely hear Sofia, even though she's standing right between my sister and me.

"Hurricanes have high winds," Sofia tells Olivia. "There's no wind here. That's all coming from a force within the water."

A force like a monster. A man-eating, angry monster. The kind of monster that helps a news kid win a best-newspaper contest.

I don't know whether to be scared or excited.

By now, a whole group of people have gathered by the lake. I look for Ms. Frogbottom in the crowd, but my teacher is nowhere to be found.

Neither is Mr. Dreich. Which is strange. This is all going on right across from his inn. You would think he'd be the first one to come out and see what's happening.

Fog-like steam rises up from the middle of the lake, making it hard to see the news crew's tiny rowboat. I can just about make it out as it struggles to stay afloat against the waves.

*SPLASH.* Oh no! The rowboat flipped over!

Mr. Dreich was right. Nessie will stop at nothing to keep from having his picture taken—even if it means drowning Millie, Amelia, and Finn in Loch Ness!

"Nessie is one mad monster!" Aiden's eyes grow wide with fear.

"I don't see anyone out there," Sofia says. She sounds worried too.

"Do you think Nessie is eating them?" Tony asks.

"Wait! There they are." Emma points toward the middle of the lake. Sure enough, through the fog I can see Amelia and Millie

bobbing up from under the surface of the lake. They are swimming hard toward the shore. But there's no sign of Finn, anywhere.

Has the Loch Ness Monster taken another victim?

For a country that has a fairy-tale unicorn as its mascot, Scotland sure is one scary place.

# 7

"THiS iS BaD," TONY MUTTERS. "BaD. BaD. Bad."

He's not wrong. This *is* bad. That monster is no joke.

"Have you seen Finn?" Millie asks Amelia frantically as the two women climb up on shore. They are both dripping wet and shivering.

"I can't see anything through that fog," Amelia answers, sounding every bit as panicked. "Nessie really didn't want us to get him on video, did he?"

"We're not getting *any* video today," Millie replies. "All the equipment is at the bottom of Loch Ness."

"Hopefully Finn's not down there too," Amelia adds nervously.

"Wait! What's that?" Olivia shouts, pointing toward the fog in the center of the lake.

"I can't tell," Aiden says. "It's too far away."

"Whatever it is, it's coming this way," Emma adds.

"I'm outta here!" Tony starts running away from the lake.

The steam begins to clear. That's when I see . . .

One hump.

Two humps.

Three humps.

*Four?* Where'd *that* hump come from?

Wait. That's not a hump. It's—

"Is that Nessie's *head*?" Aiden asks nervously. "I think I see red hair."

"Do you think Nessie can get to us if we're on the shore?" Olivia takes a few steps back.

"Maybe we should go into the inn," Emma suggests in fear.

"No." My throat is so dry, I can hardly get the word out. I'm scared too. But I'm not leaving. I've been waiting all day for this.

"That's not Nessie's head," Millie corrects Aiden. "It's Finn's."

"Finn *and* Nessie!" I add excitedly. "They're together!"

"I don't think that's Nessie." Sofia tells us.

"You mean there's *another* monster in Loch Ness?" I ask her.

Sofia shakes her head. "I mean it's not a monster. I think it's a log."

"A log with three humps?"

Sofia shrugs. "It's a lumpy log."

"It can't be," I insist. "You saw those waves. There was no wind. *Something* had to have caused that."

"The water was literally pulling us," Amelia tells Sofia. "What else besides Nessie would be that powerful?"

"That pull was *monstrously* strong," Millie adds.

My sister giggles. "Good one."

"I wasn't joking," Millie insists.

"Here he comes!" Amelia points to Finn. He's swimming in our direction.

"He climbed off the monster's back!" Millie cheers.

"It's not the Loch Ness Mon—" Sofia begins.

"I can't believe Nessie just let him go like that," I say, cutting her off midsentence.

"Maybe Nessie wanted to scare us away but not hurt anyone," Amelia suggests. "Just like with that fisherman. Nessie tipped the boat, but he let the man get away."

"That doesn't sound like monster behavior," Sofia points out.

"Finn! Are you okay?" Millie asks as he crawls onto the shore from the lake. He's out of breath, and too weak to even walk.

"How'd you get Nessie to free you?" Amelia asks. "Did you fight him off?"

Finn rests his head on his knees and frowns. "That wasn't Nessie. It was just a hollow log. I floated on it till I got my strength."

Sofia smiles knowingly.

"A *log*?" Millie repeats. "We lost all that equipment for a *log*?"

Millie isn't the only one who's disappointed. The people gathered by the lake are leaving now. Loch Ness is calm again. There's nothing left to see.

"I'm freezing. Do we have any dry jackets?" Finn asks.

"Maybe in the van," Amelia answers. "Come on. We have to get back to the newsroom." She sounds bummed.

"We're going to be in trouble with our station manager," Millie says. "And all for nothing."

"You can't go," I tell them. "*Something* caused that storm. What about the steam? It could have been Nessie's hot breath."

"Forget it, laddie," Amelia tells me. "There's no story there."

"No story there." The three words no news kid ever wants to hear.

But she's said them. A moment later Amelia, Millie, and Finn are back in the van and driving off . . . *on the wrong side of the road*. They must have been really upset to make a mistake like that!

"Is everything okay?" Tony shouts from the grassy area away from the shore.

---

## FROGBOTTOM FACTS

★ People in Scotland drive on the left side of the road. It's not the wrong side. It's just different from in the United States, where people drive on the right.

★ In Scottish cars the steering wheel is on the right-hand side, unlike in the United States, where the wheel is on the left.

---

No. Everything is *not* okay. I'm sure that storm was caused by the Loch Ness Monster. But I don't know how to prove it.

"You can come back. You were scared off by a giant log," I call back grumpily.

"You sure are being mean to Tony," Olivia tells me. "What did he ever do to you?"

When the meanest teaser in the class tells you to quit being mean, you probably should quit. Especially since at the moment it's not really Tony I'm mad at.

I'm angry with the Loch Ness Monster for not showing us his face.

"I'm sorry," I say to Tony as he walks back over to where the rest of us are standing. "I shouldn't have made fun. It's not your fault you're scared of everything."

"I'm not scared of everything!" Tony insists.

"Okay, not *everything*," I agree. "But a lot of stuff. Like heights, and horses, and—"

"Speaking of horses," Olivia interrupts. "Look over there."

A small black horse with a white spot on its head is trotting across the road toward us.

"I'll show you I'm not scared!" Tony says as he runs toward the horse.

"You don't have to prove anything!" I call. But either he can't hear me or he's not listening, because the next thing I know, he's petting the horse on its nose.

Wow. For Tony that's a huge deal.

"Hey, isn't that the same black horse we saw before?" Olivia asks.

"I think so," Emma agrees. "It has that patch of white fur on its head."

A patch of white in the middle of a head of black hair . . . *I've seen that somewhere.*

Wait a minute.

I can't believe I didn't think of this before.

"Does that horse remind you of Mr. Dreich?" I ask. "Look at its head. It's all black except for that white patch."

"Now that you mention it, yeah," Sofia agrees.

"Don't you guys think it's strange that this horse has shown up where we are, twice now?" I continue.

"It likes us," Emma suggests.

"Maybe," I say. "But how did it know we'd be at the castle? Or that we'd be coming back to the inn?"

"What are you trying to say?" Olivia asks me.

"Mr. Dreich heard us talking about going to the castle," I point out. "And he had to figure we'd come back here sooner or later for a snack. I mean, he's met Aiden."

Aiden grins and pats his hungry belly.

"So you think Mr. Dreich talks *horse*?" My sister looks at me like I'm nuts.

But I'm not. I'm onto something.

"We never saw Mr. Dreich's feet," I point out. "He had those huge rain boots on all the time. Even inside. We couldn't tell if he had feet or—"

"Oliver, you don't actually think—" Olivia begins.

"It *couldn't* be," Sofia insists.

"Maybe it could," Aiden suggests.

"He sounded funny when he walked,"

Emma remembers. *"Clip-clop, clip-clop. Kind of like a horse."*

*Kind of like a horse.* That's enough proof for me.

"TONY! RUN AWAY!" I shout. "THAT HORSE IS MR. DREICH! IT'S A KELPIE!"

## WE WATCH AS THE MR. DREICH HORSE

gently lowers itself to the ground and lets
Tony climb onto its back.

I can't believe what I'm seeing. Tony is
petrified of horses. I know that because
when we went to the petting zoo in first
grade, he refused to feed them. He stayed
in the rabbit pen instead—until an especially big bunny scared him off.

"Tony! Don't!" I cry out.

But it's too late. Tony has already climbed up there.

My heart is pounding. Tony is on the back of a kelpie. *And it's all my fault.*

"If I hadn't been so mean to him, none of this would be happening," I say. "I got too caught up in winning that newspaper contest. Instead of thinking about meeting Scoop Schaeffer, I should have been thinking about Tony's feelings."

"The kelpie isn't moving," Aiden points out. "Tony can't get in any trouble on a kelpie that's still."

"And it's so little," Emma adds. "Tony could jump off if the kelpie starts to move."

"We don't even know for sure that it *is* a kelpie," Sofia reminds us. "You could be interpreting the facts incorrectly. I, for one, still think kelpies are just old Scottish folktales."

That's all true. And surprisingly, Tony doesn't look *too* scared. He's petting the horse. This could be good for him. He's overcoming his fear.

I may have done Tony a favor.

"WHOA!" Suddenly Tony lets out a cry. I watch in horror as the horse stands up and starts galloping. "STOP, HORSE!"

The horse doesn't stop. It just keeps running, right toward the lake.

Tony isn't wearing a life jacket. Tony *needs* a life jacket. He's a lousy swimmer. *I've got to save him!*

The next thing I know, I'm running after that horse.

I mean running after Mr. Dreich.

I mean . . .

I don't know *what* I mean. All I know is that no matter how fast I run, I'll never catch a galloping horse.

So before I can do anything to stop

it, the horse has dragged my friend into Loch Ness!

*Uh-oh!*

There's no way I'm going back to school without Tony. What would we tell his mother at pickup? "Your kid has been eaten by a horse, who is really a man"? Or a man, who is really a horse?

Either way, she's not going to be happy.

I kick off my shoes and start toward the lake.

"Oliver, what are you doing?" Olivia asks.

"I got my advanced beginner swim badge at camp last summer," I remind her. "I'm going to swim Tony out of the lake before he becomes a kelpie lunch."

"Ms. Frogbottom isn't going to like this," Aiden says. "She'll be back any minute with those snacks. Maybe you should wait."

"There's no time," I argue. "I have to do this, even if Ms. Frogbottom gets so mad that she sends a note home to my mother."

My stomach is flipping and flopping nervously. I wonder if this is how Tony feels all the time. I hope not. It's awful.

But I'm not going to let being scared keep me from doing what I have to do.

"Here I go!" I start walking into the waters of Loch Ness. "Yikes! That's cold!"

"Oliver! Wait!" I hear my sister yelling behind me. "Look!"

Whoa! As if things weren't bad enough . . .

A giant head pokes out of the water. It looks kind of like a dinosaur in a museum. It's him. *It's the Loch Ness Monster!*

## FROGBOTTOM FACTS

★ People probably shouldn't swim in Loch Ness—not because of a monster but because the water is so cold. It stays at about 42 degrees Fahrenheit all year long. That's only 10 degrees above freezing.

# 9

"YI–I–I–KES!"

A moment later I hear a shout as something—or someone—comes shooting out of the lake.

It's Tony! He's flying through the air. And then . . .

*THUMP!*

He lands right on the head of the Loch Ness Monster!

Nessie's eyes blink with surprise.

He opens his giant jaws. *Wide.*

Oh no! It looks like the Loch Ness Monster is going to eat Tony!

*HONK!* The monster lets out a cry so loud, it shakes the ground beneath me. He sure sounds mad. Tony's in real trouble.

Then Nessie starts swimming right toward us. Now I think we're *all* in trouble.

I'm so scared that the hairs on my arms are standing straight up.

"Jump, Tony!" I shout. "Get off that monster's head before he eats you!"

"I can't." Tony's voice is shaking. "I'm too high up."

The Loch Ness Monster lowers his

head to the nearby shore. He stares at us.

We stare back, frozen with fear.

Then Tony climbs down from Nessie's head and steps onto the slippery stones.

*It's unbelievable.*

"I think the Loch Ness Monster just saved your life," Aiden tells him.

Tony takes a deep breath. He checks his fingers. Maybe to make sure they're all still there.

"He did." Tony sounds as surprised as the rest of us. "That kelpie would have eaten me if it hadn't been scared off by Nessie. The horse took one look at him and leaped away as hard as it could."

"Like an underwater bucking bronco?" Aiden asks him.

"Yup. The horse bucked so hard, I flew off. Right into the air."

"Weren't you scared?" I ask him.

Tony nods. "Sure. But probably not as scared as Nessie. I doubt he was expecting a kid to suddenly land on top of his head."

Nessie opens his mouth and lets out another mighty *HONK!* Then he dives and swims back into the dark waters of Loch Ness.

I guess Nessie wasn't mad after all. Honking must just be how he talks.

"When that horse dragged you under, I was so scared," I tell Tony.

"How do you think *I* felt?" Tony replies.

"Who knew the Loch Ness Monster

could actually be a hero?" Emma says.

"I can't wait to get back to school and write about it for the *4A Gazette*!" I exclaim.

"No way, Oliver," Tony insists. "You can't tell *anyone* that Nessie is real."

"What are you talking about?" I ask him. "Of course I can. We just saw him. You just *rode* him!"

"You heard what Mr. Dreich said," Tony explains. "If people think the Loch Ness Monster is real, they'll come looking for him. I don't think he wants to be seen. You saw what he did to those reporters. And I know how badly he scared that kelpie. It hasn't come back. I bet Nessie is eating it right now."

"I wonder why Nessie didn't hurt *you*," Sofia says.

"A monster probably knows another monster when he sees one," Tony says. "That kelpie was a bad dude. But I'm not."

"The reporters weren't monsters," I argue. "They just wanted their big story. Imagine how Finn, Millie, and Amelia are going to feel when they find out they've been scooped by a news *kid*. After I write this article, they'll have to admit I'm as much of a reporter as they are."

"You can't write that story, Liver," Olivia says. "The Loch Ness Monster protected Tony. We should protect the Loch Ness Monster."

"But this is the biggest—" I begin.

My classmates frown.

"Don't forget that visit from Scoop Schaeffer," I try.

Olivia shakes her head.

*Ugh*. I hate when my sister does this. And I don't mean calling me "Liver." I hate when she's right and I'm wrong.

"Okay," I agree finally. "But now we don't have a powerful front-page story. We'll never win that visit from Scoop Schaeffer."

"Maybe not," Tony agrees. "But we can still put out a good newspaper. I know how we can add some excitement to it."

"How?"

"I'll show you when we get back." Tony looks down at his wet clothes. "Yuck. Nothing feels more gross than wet sneakers."

"You'll dry off by the end of the school day," Olivia tells him.

"Speaking of school, where's Ms. Frogbottom?" Aiden wonders. "I hope she gets back with those snacks soon. I'm—"

I don't hear the rest of what Aiden is saying because his voice is drowned out by some strange, high-pitched, loud music. It's a sad sound, with notes that go up and down and pile on top of one another without stopping.

"Whoa! Check out Ms. Frogbottom," Olivia shouts over the music.

"I don't know about that fur hat," Emma says loudly, "but her plaid skirt is cute."

"The skirt is called a kilt," Sofia tells her. "And the plaid pattern is called a tartan."

"Forget her clothes," Tony says. "What's that thing she's blowing into?"

Ms. Frogbottom breathes into a long tube attached to what looks like a big balloon. She uses her fingers to cover some holes at the bottom of a different  tube. Our teacher hits a few more notes and finishes her song.

Everyone claps.

"Thank you," Ms. Frogbottom says, taking a little bow. "It's been a while since I played the bagpipes. I forgot how much wind it takes."

Our teacher glances at Tony. "Oh my," she says, pulling a big fluffy towel out of her backpack. "Better dry yourself off."

"Did you bring back any food?" Aiden interrupts. "My stomach is telling me it must be afternoon snack time."

"Your stomach is correct," Ms. Frogbottom replies. "I would have loved to get you fresh-baked scones, but I can't find Mr. Dreich. Have any of you seen him?"

We all look at one another. We're not sure what to say.

"There are crackers and juice in the classroom," Ms. Frogbottom continues as she shoves her big furry hat and bagpipes into her backpack and pulls out the Magic Map. "We do need to get back. I'm just sorry we didn't get to go out for a ride on the lovely waters of Loch Ness."

I'm not sorry. I've already seen what's going on in that lake. It's not all that lovely.

Ms. Frogbottom points to Left Turn Alleyway Elementary on the map. Suddenly a white light flashes all around us. My body feels weightless, and I think my feet have just left the ground.

It's like I'm flying in space. And then . . .

## FROGBOTTOM FACTS

★ Bagpipes have been played for at least 1,900 years. The instrument was mentioned in ancient Greek and Latin writings from about 100 AD.

"WOW, TONY," I SAY TO MY PAL LATER that day when we're back in our classroom. "That looks amazing."

"I told you I would come up with something exciting for the *4A Gazette*," Tony answers.

Tony and Olivia are working on their new comic strip, *Super Kid and the Underwater Monster*. It's about a fourth grader who travels around on the head

of a giant monster that lives in a lake.

The kid in the comic strip looks a whole lot like Tony. But hey, if Tony wants to turn himself into a superhero, it's fine with me. He is the only one of us who actually rode on the head of the Loch Ness Monster.

It really stinks that we can't write about any of that in our newspaper. Not even the kelpie part. We don't know for sure that the horse was actually Mr. Dreich. If we aren't 100 percent sure he was a kel-pie, then we can't print an article about it.

"I almost forgot," Ms. Frogbottom announces suddenly. "We have a new class pet!"

I look around the classroom. There's no sign of a hamster, a guinea pig, or even a goldfish.

"Meet Veronica." Ms. Frogbottom reaches into her backpack and pulls out a very strange-looking plant.

"Our class pet is a *plant*?" Aiden asks.

"Veronica's not just any plant." Ms. Frogbottom points to the sharp things that kind of look like teeth. "She's a Venus flytrap."

"But plants are *boring*," Emma blurts out.

Ms. Frogbottom shoots her a look.

"No offense," Emma says.

"None taken," our teacher replies. "But I disagree."

"Having a Venus flytrap in the classroom is going to be interesting," Sofia insists.

"How?" I wonder. "You can't pet it or play with it."

"You can feed it," Sofia explains.

"You mean *water* it," Aiden corrects her.

Sofia shakes her head. "Venus flytraps are carnivorous. Which means—"

"They eat meat," Tony finishes her sentence. "Like carnivorous dinosaurs."

"You can take turns feeding Veronica," Ms. Frogbottom tells us.

"What does she eat?" Olivia asks.

"Mostly bugs." Sofia has already looked up Venus flytraps on her tablet. "Crickets, ants, grasshoppers, and beetles."

Hmmm . . . that is kind of cool, actually.

"Imagine the experiments we can do," Sofia continues. "We can see if Veronica responds to music. Scientists believe plants react to classical—"

"That's it!" I shout, interrupting the class brain.

"*What's* it?" Olivia asks me.

"Our front-page news story. It will be about Veronica, the meat-eating plant. No other class at Left Turn Alleyway Elementary has a pet like her."

"Can I write the article?" Sofia asks me.

"Definitely!" I tell her. "And be sure to

take pictures of Veronica eating." I turn to my teacher. "It's okay to take pictures in the classroom, right?"

Ms. Frogbottom smiles and nods.

"Great!" I exclaim.

Sofia isn't the only person excited about Veronica now. I'm pretty psyched too. This is going to be a great story. It might even help us win that contest.

But if it doesn't, the article will teach our readers something they didn't know before, which is exactly what newspapers are supposed to do.

"How was school today?" our babysitter, Jessie, asks Olivia and me as we walk home later that afternoon.

"We got a lot of work done on our class newspaper," I tell Jessie.

"And we went on another field trip," Olivia adds.

"Yeah," I say. "I guess you could say it was just a regular day in class 4A."

# WORDS YOU HEAR ON A FIELD TRIP TO SCOTLAND

**bagpipes:** A musical instrument that is made of a tube, a bag for air, and pipes from which the sound comes

**blood pudding:** A sausage made of pork blood, pork fat or beef fat, and oatmeal, oat groats, or barley groats; also called "blood sausage"

**carnivore:** An animal that primarily eats other animals

**clan:** A group of closely related families, often from the Scottish Highlands

**herbivore:** An animal that eats only plants

**kilt:** A knee-length pleated skirt-like garment with a plaid pattern, traditionally worn by men but now worn by girls and women as well

**loch:** The Scottish Gaelic word for a lake

**loom:** A frame or machine used for weaving thread or yarn to make cloth

**rumbledethumps:** A traditional side dish from the Scottish borders; it usually includes potatoes and cabbage

**scone:** A small biscuit-like cake made with flour, fat, milk, sweetener, and sometimes added fruit

**tartan:** A plaid pattern made of stripes of different widths and colors; Scottish clans have their own tartan patterns